The Lost Tickets

Story by Neil Griffiths

Illustrated by Lisa Williams

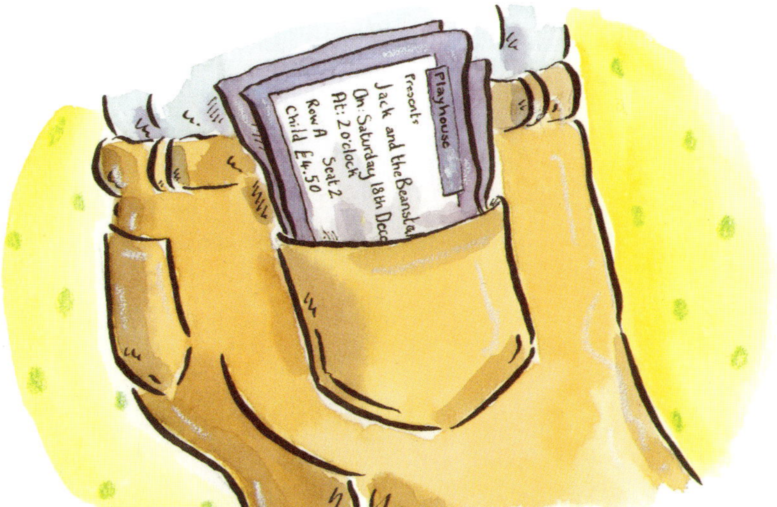

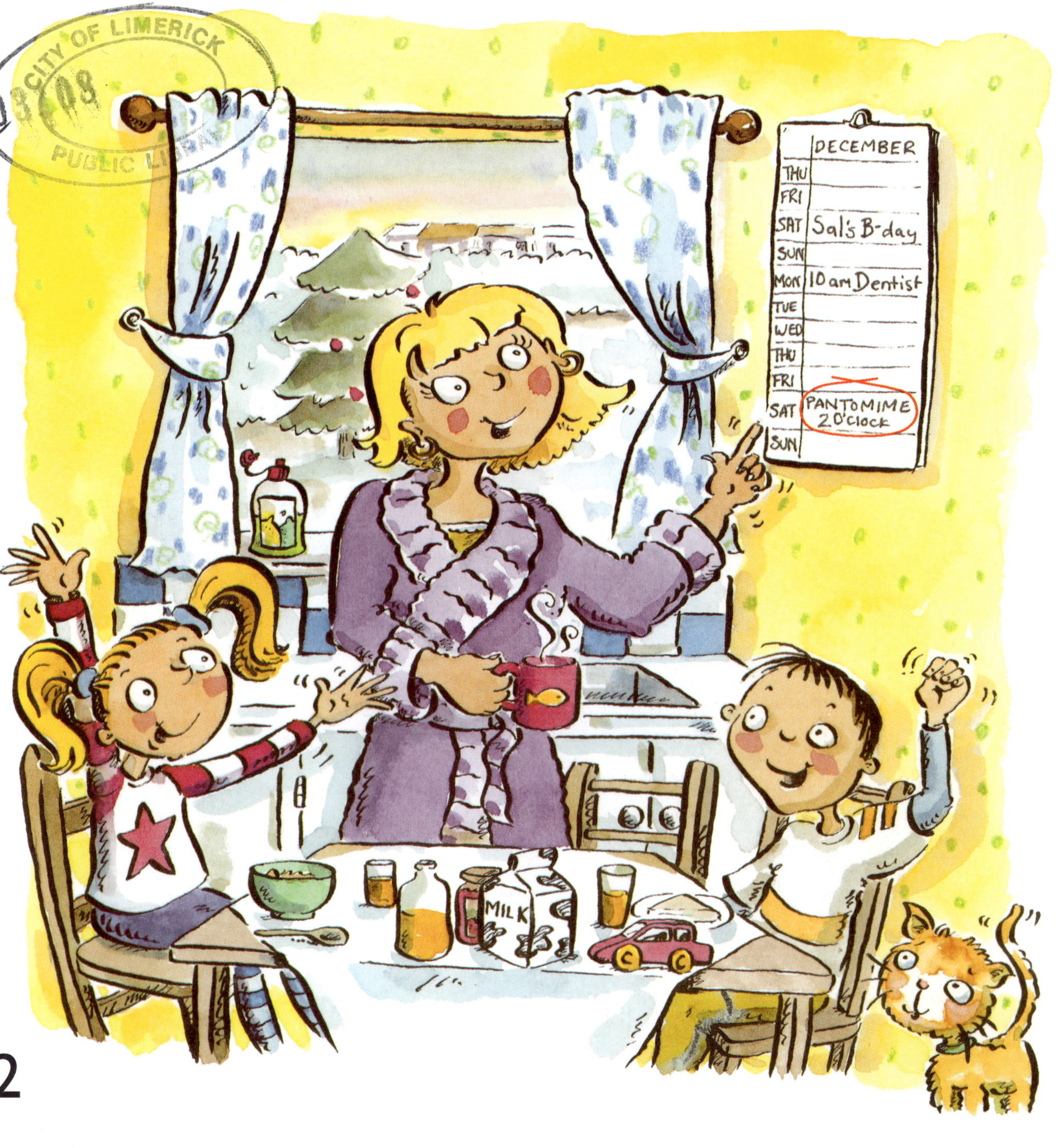
DECEMBER
THU
FRI
SAT Sal's B-day
SUN
MON 10 am Dentist
TUE
WED
THU
FRI
SAT PANTOMIME 2 O'clock
SUN
MILK

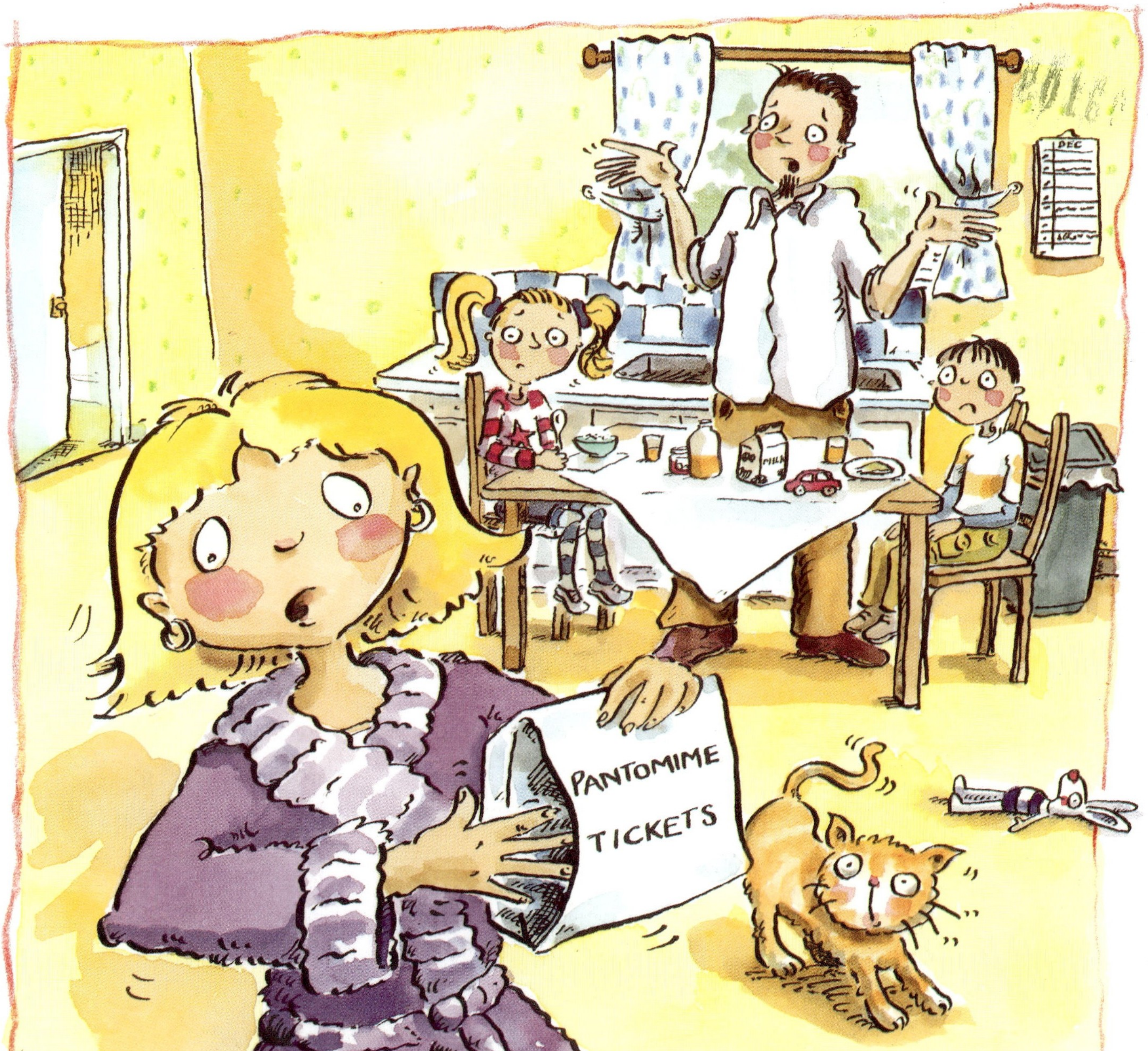
DEC
PANTOMIME
TICKETS

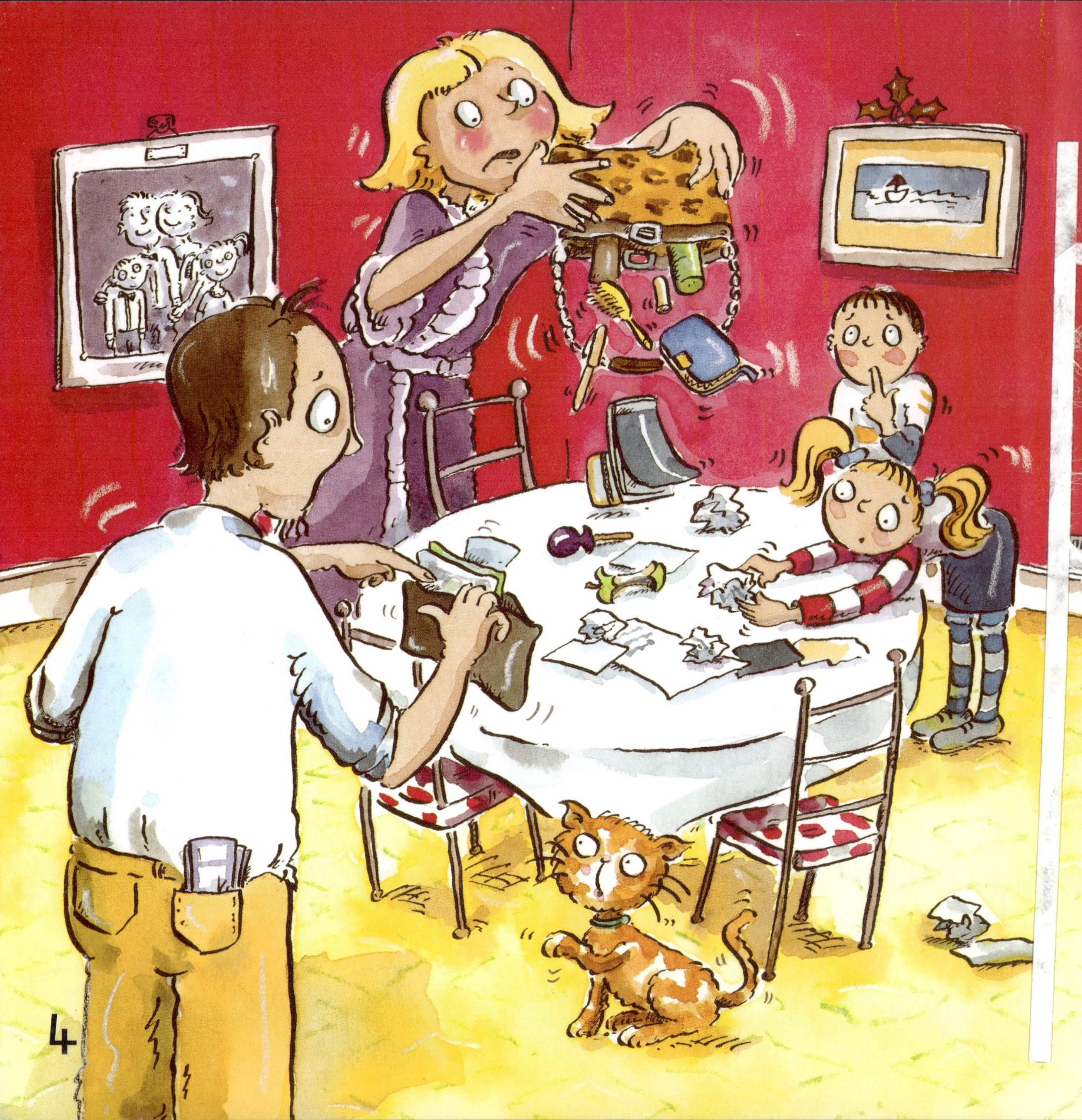

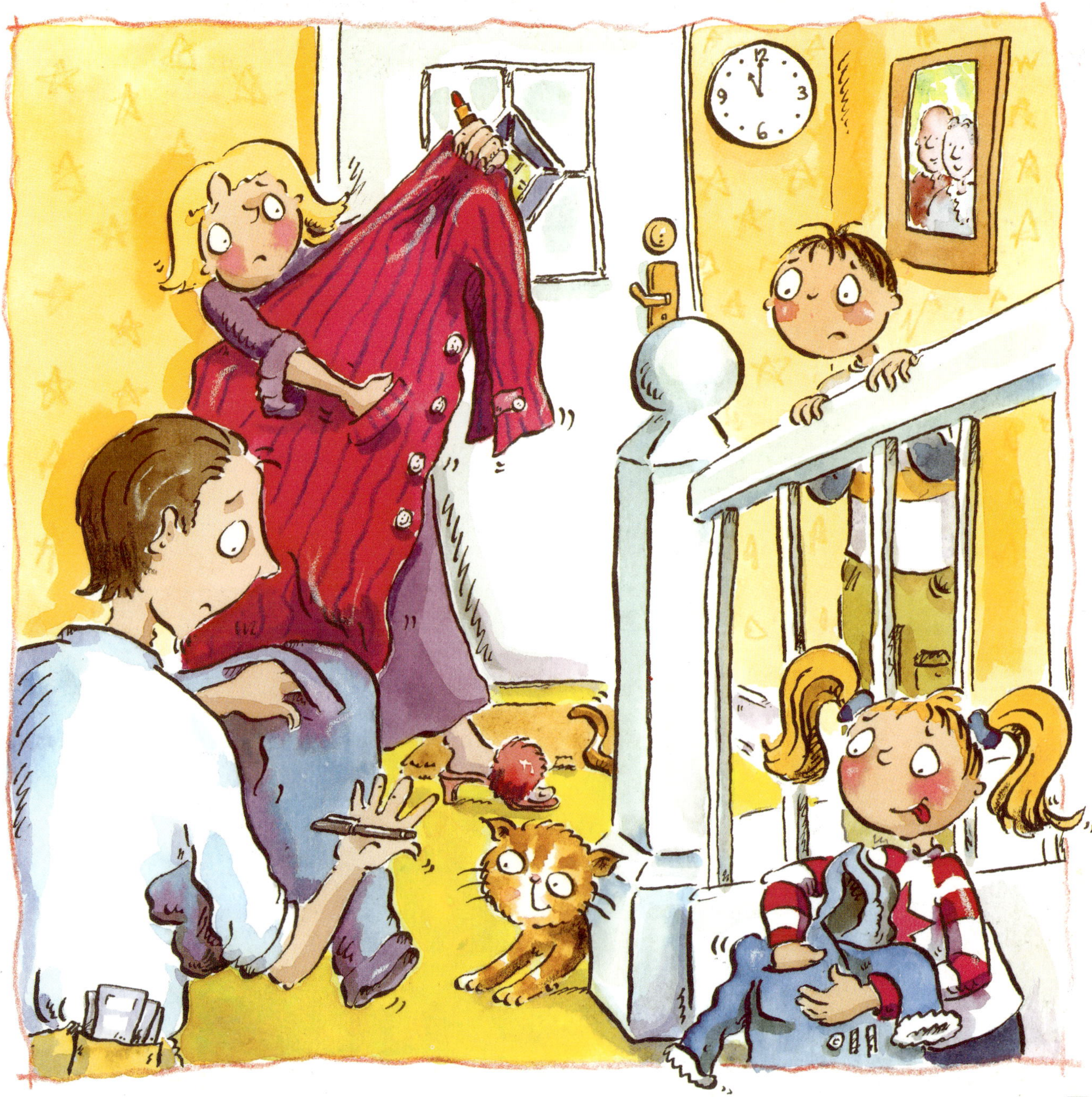

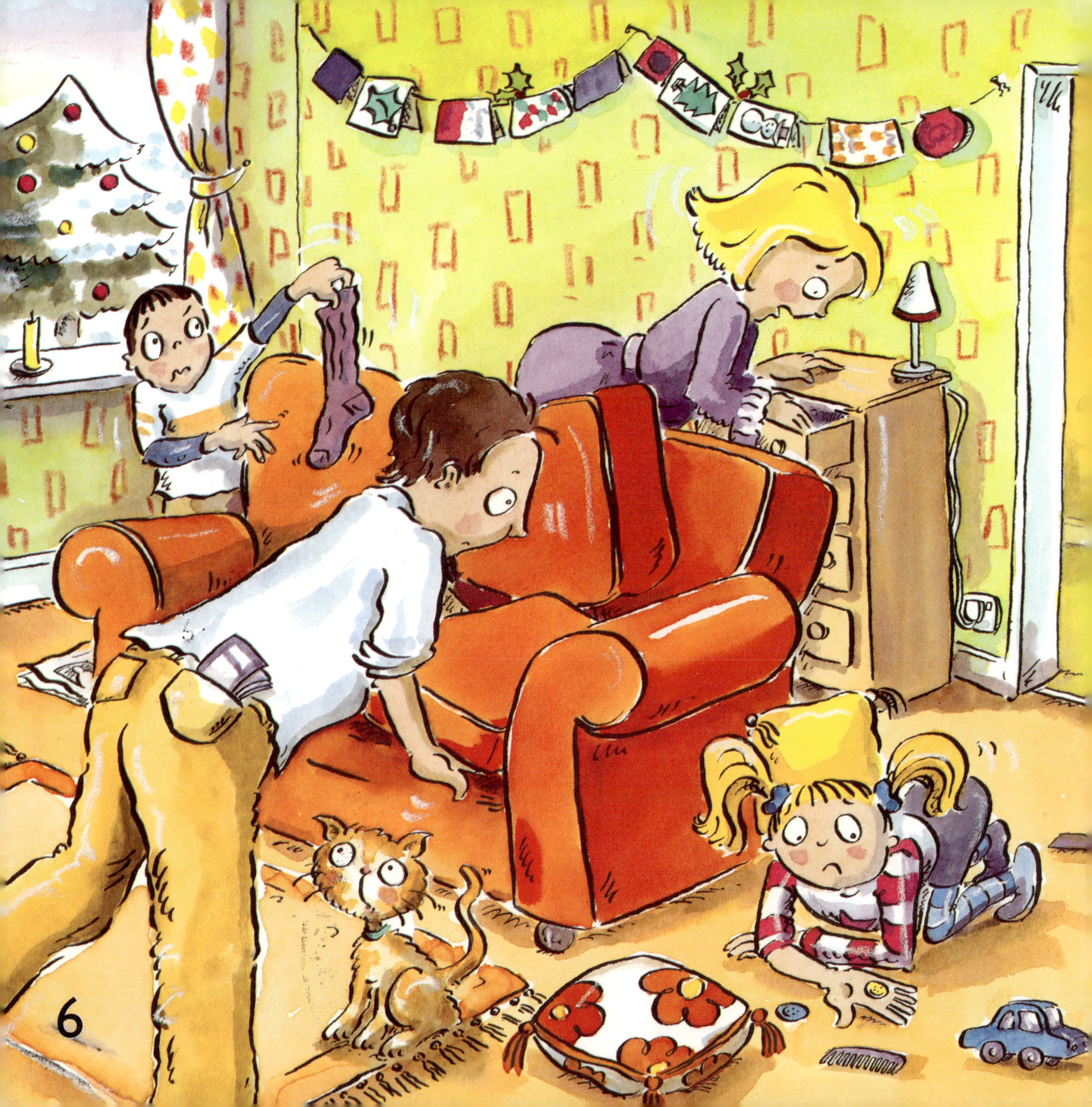

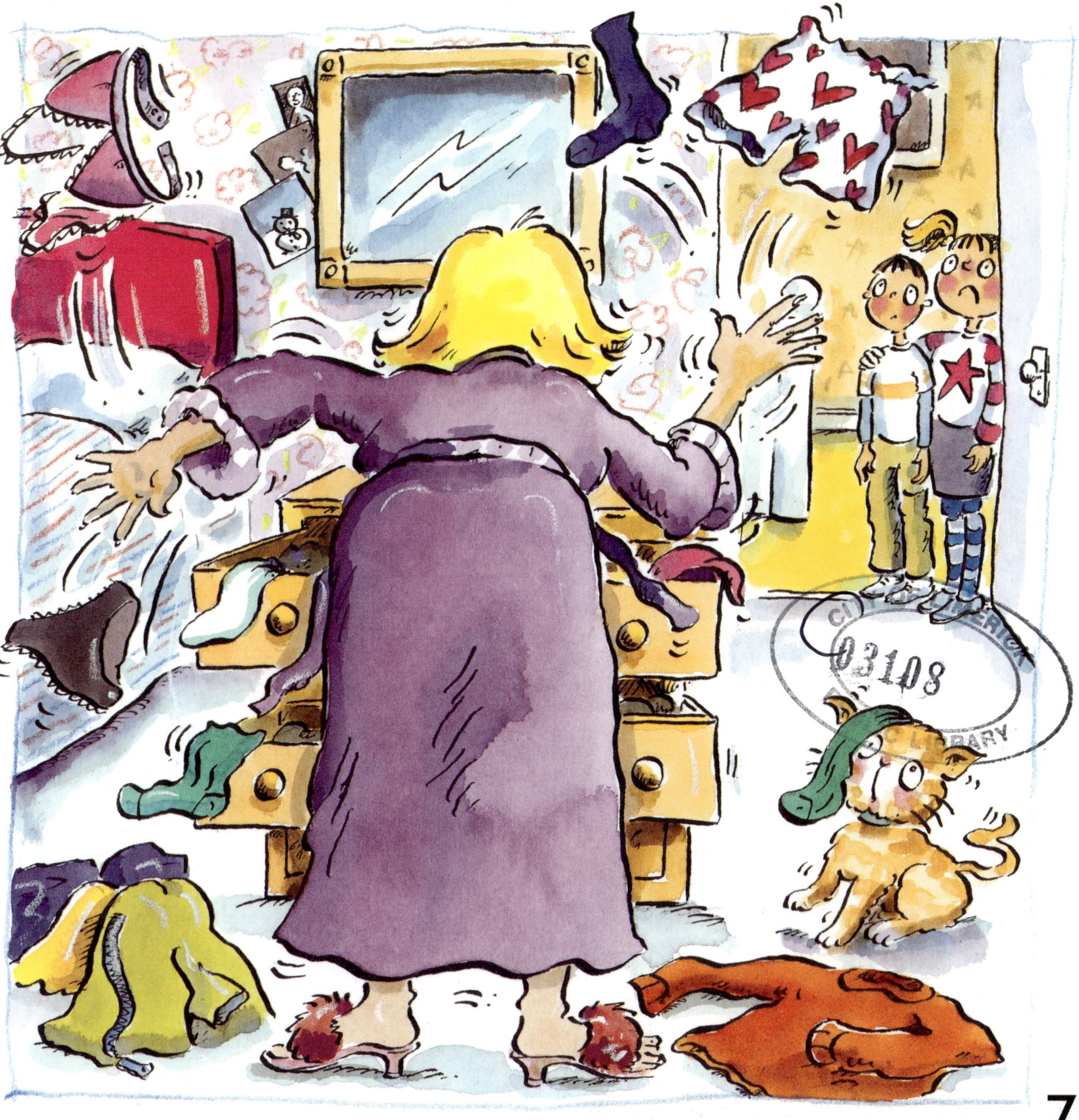

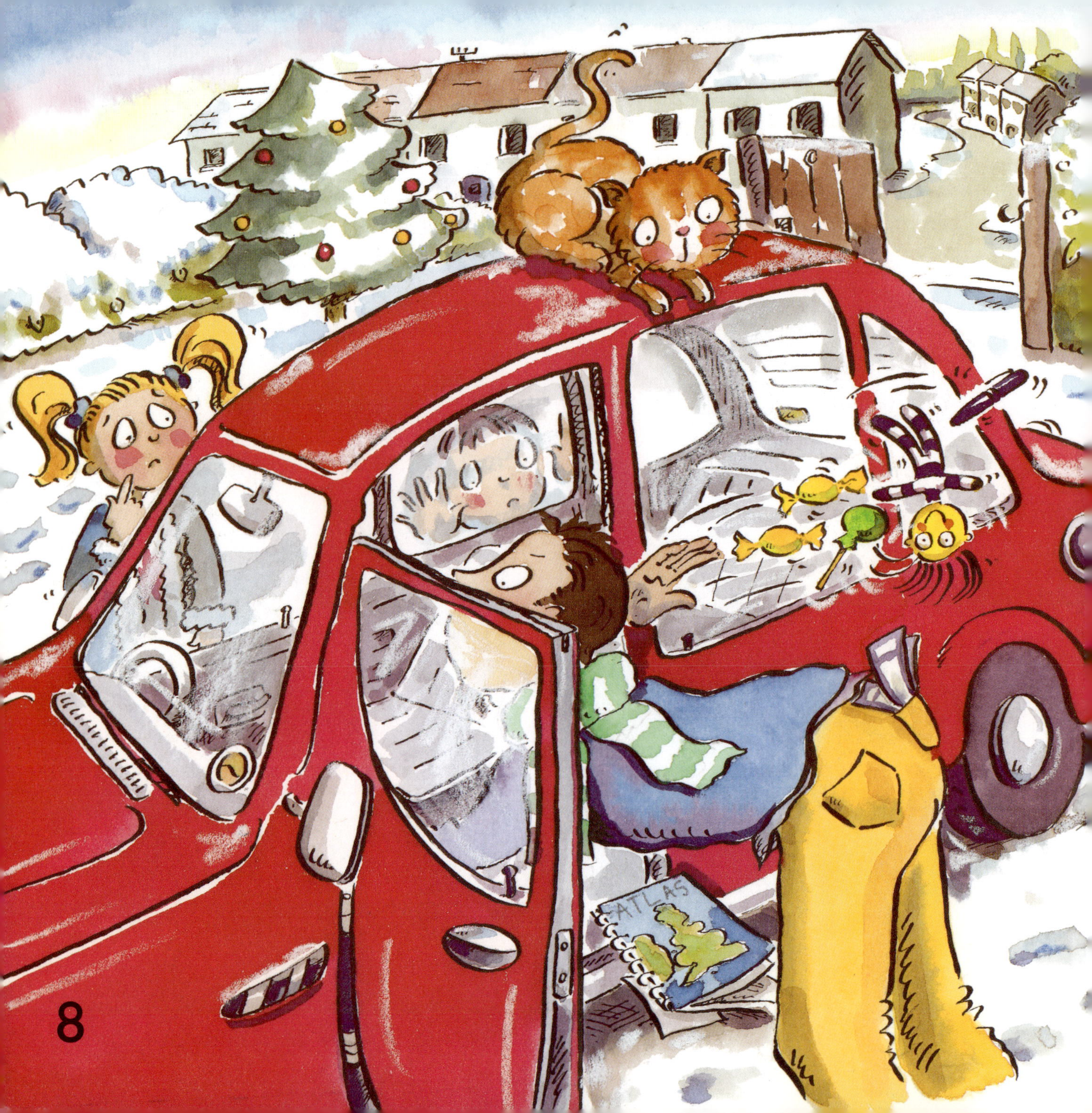
ATLAS

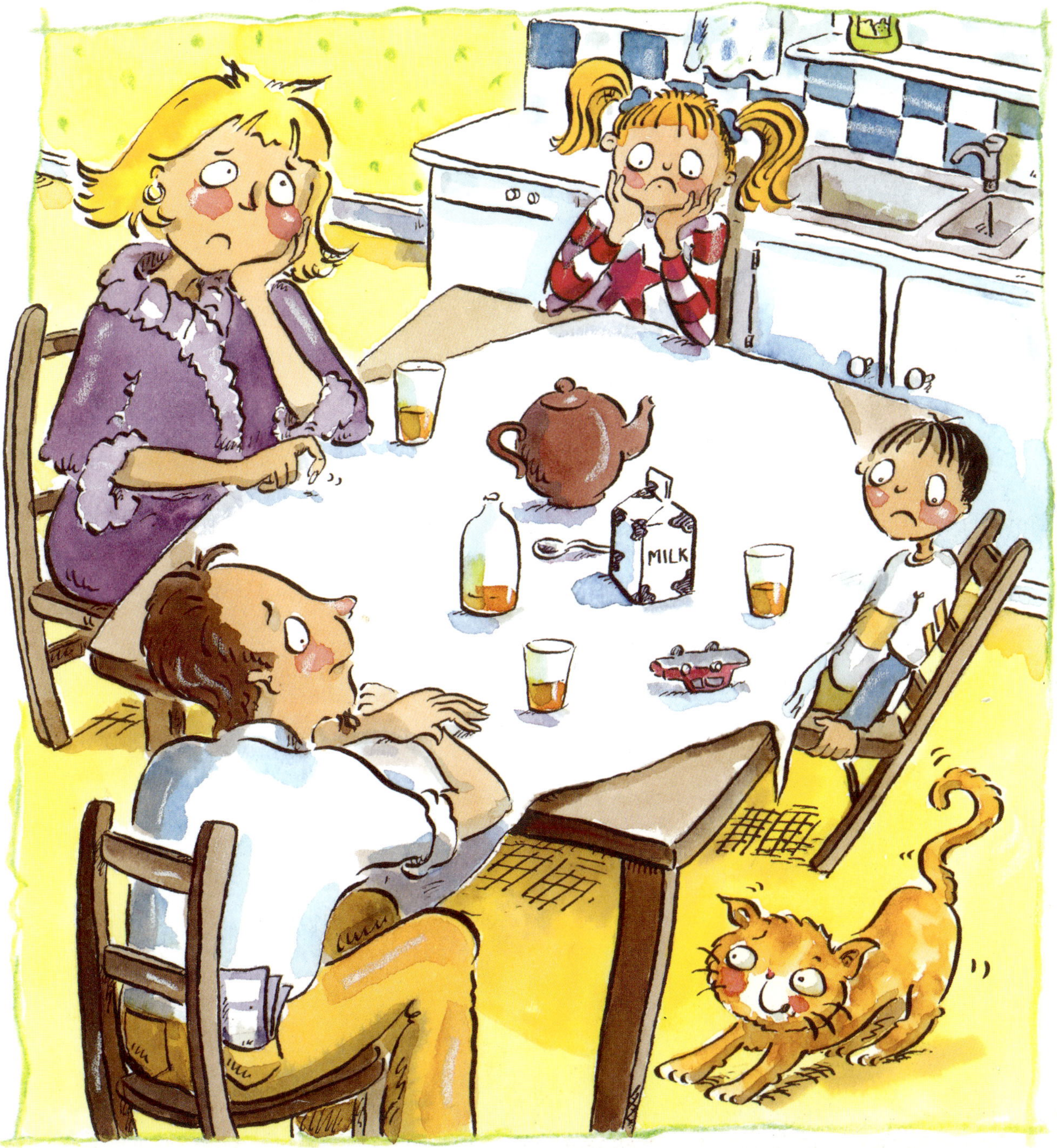
MILK

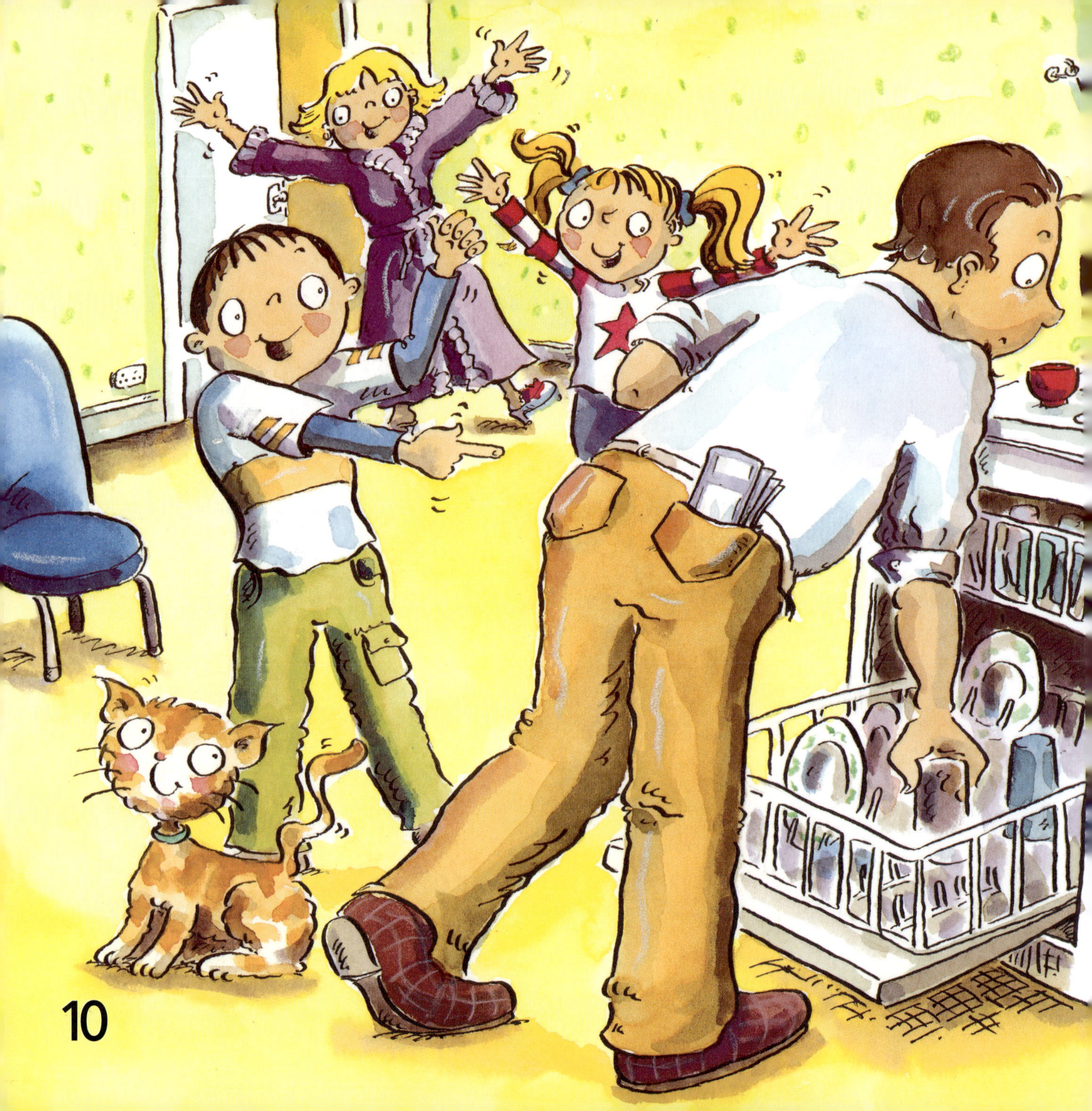

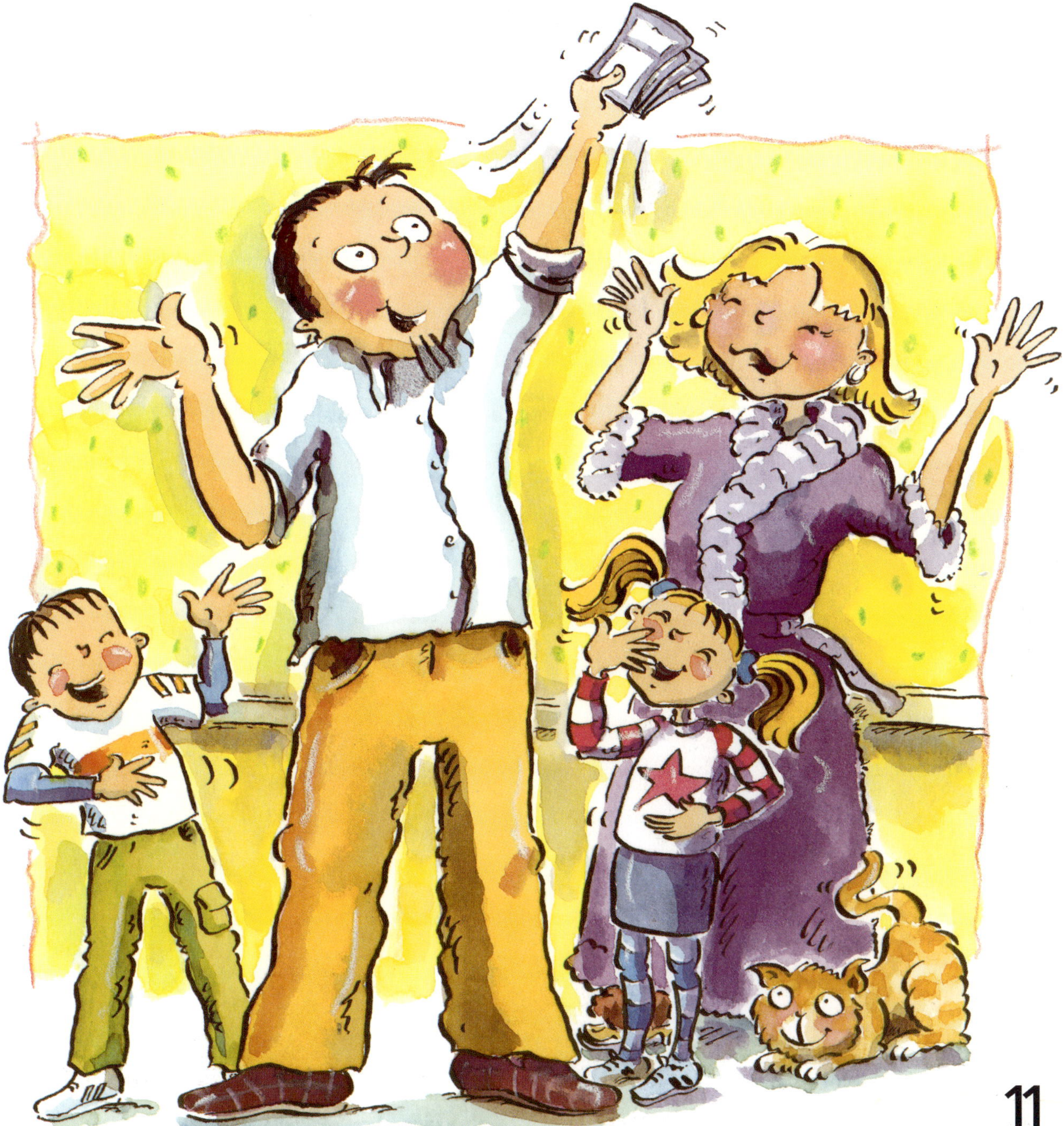

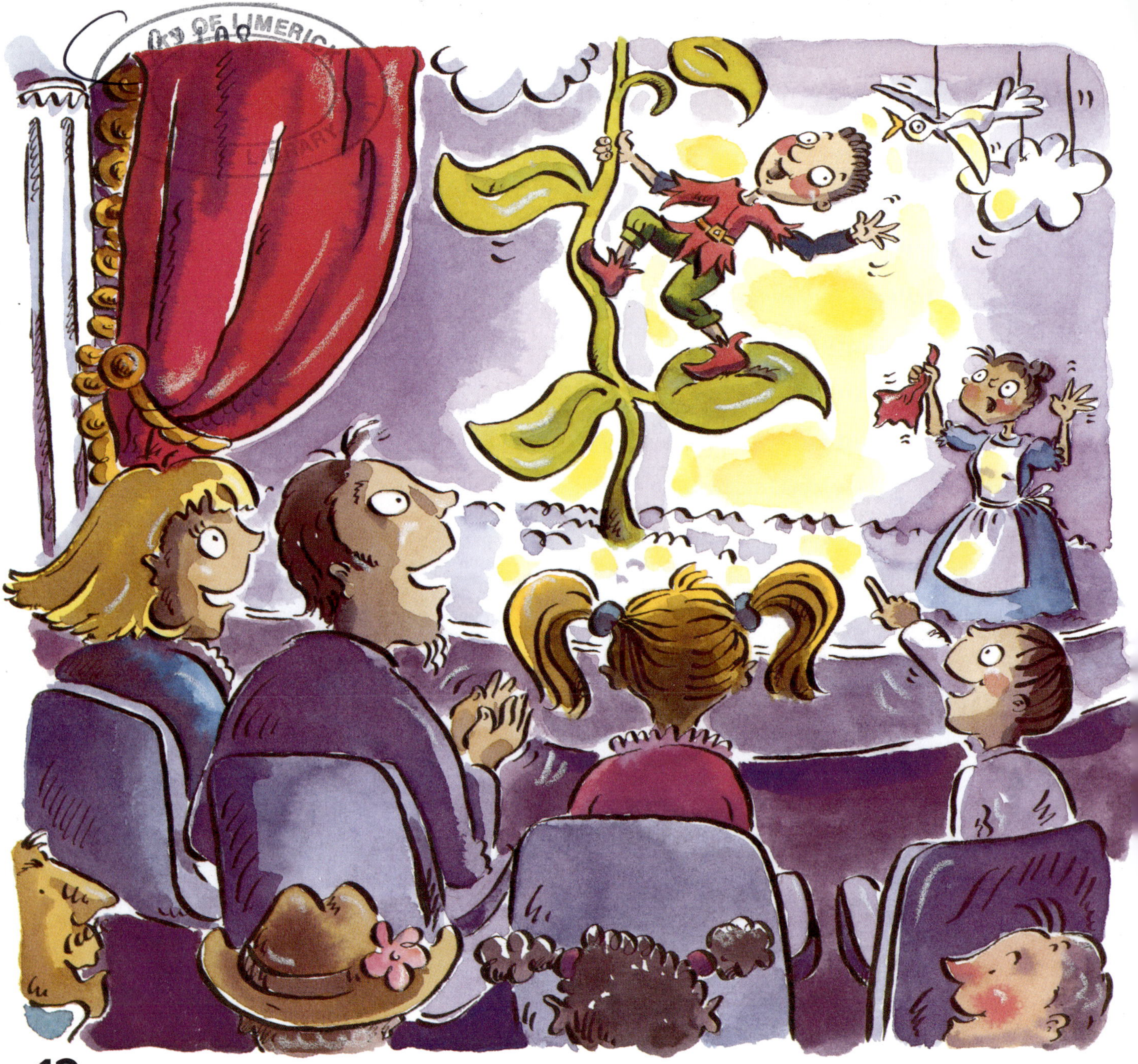